**Put Beginning Readers on the Right Track with
ALL ABOARD READING™**

The All Aboard Reading series is especially designed for beginning readers. Written by noted authors and illustrated in full color, these are books that children really want to read—books to excite their imagination, expand their interests, make them laugh, and support their feelings. With fiction and nonfiction stories that are high interest and curriculum-related, All Aboard Reading books offer something for every young reader. And with four different reading levels, the All Aboard Reading series lets you choose which books are most appropriate for your children and their growing abilities.

Picture Readers
Picture Readers have super-simple texts, with many nouns appearing as rebus pictures. At the end of each book are 24 flash cards—on one side is a rebus picture; on the other side is the written-out word.

Station Stop 1
Station Stop 1 books are best for children who have just begun to read. Simple words and big type make these early reading experiences more comfortable. Picture clues help children to figure out the words on the page. Lots of repetition throughout the text helps children to predict the next word or phrase—an essential step in developing word recognition.

Station Stop 2
Station Stop 2 books are written specifically for children who are reading with help. Short sentences make it easier for early readers to understand what they are reading. Simple plots and simple dialogue help children with reading comprehension.

Station Stop 3
Station Stop 3 books are perfect for children who are reading alone. With longer text and harder words, these books appeal to children who have mastered basic reading skills. More complex stories captivate children who are ready for more challenging books.

In addition to All Aboard Reading books, look for All Aboard Math Readers™ (fiction stories that teach math concepts children are learning in school); All Aboard Science Readers™ (nonfiction books that explore the most fascinating science topics in age-appropriate language); and All Aboard Poetry Readers™ (funny, rhyming poems for readers of all levels).

All Aboard for happy reading!

ISBN 978-0-545-52830-6

12 11 10 9 8 7 6 5 4 3 2 1   12 13 14 15 16 17/0

Printed in the U.S.A.   40

First Scholastic printing, December 2012

All Aboard Reading™

SkippyjonJones

THE GREAT BEAN CAPER

Based on the *Skippyjon Jones* series created by

J U D Y   S C H A C H N E R

SCHOLASTIC INC.

 bounced up and

down on his big-boy .

As he bounced he said,

"Oh, I'm Skippyjon Jones,

and I bounce with the best.

No one dares cross me,

I'll beat any pest."

Then  began to

dig through his ⬛ .

Out came a ⬤ and a

🚗 . Finally, he found

what he was looking for . . .

Skippyjon put on his  and tied on

his ⌒◯ꝗ. Then he

walked toward his ▮ .

Inside, a  hissed. A  squeaked. And Los Chimichangos waited for Skippyjon. "Ay, Skippito," said Don Diego, a purple  . "It is good you are here. El Bumblebeeto has stolen our  !"

"Holy guacamole!"

Skippito Friskito cried.

"We must get them back!"  grabbed his

and an ⟨image⟩. And off the

muchachos went in his

 .

" 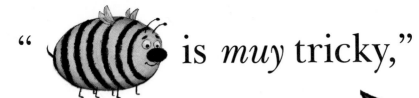 is *muy* tricky,"

Don Diego said. But

wasn't worried.

"There are **8** of us, and

just **1** of him," Skippito

Friskito said as the

sailed down the 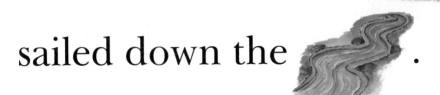 .

"Keep a lookout, *perritos!*"

At last the *muchachos*

reached an  . A

trail of  led away

from the water. *"Vamanos!"*

cried Skippito.

Skippito and his *amigos*

found  resting in a

 . "Ay, Bumblebeeto,"

Skippito called out, "give

Los Chimichangos back

their  !" But El

Bumblebeeto didn't hear

him. He was asleep!

Skippito quietly climbed

up the . Then he

began to pile the

into his . Suddenly,

El Bumblebeeto opened

his .

 grabbed the

and raced down the

. Los Chimichangos

chanted, "Skippito is a

hero!" But  just kept

running. He was in such a

hurry to get away that he

crashed right into . . .

Mama Junebug Jones.

"Come on, Mr. Fuzzy Pants,"  said. "Let's go get some dinner. I made  !"

bed/*cama*

Skippyjon
Jones

ball/*pelota*

toy chest/
caja de juguete

cape/*capa*

car/*coche*

closet/*armario*

mask/
máscara

mouse/*ratón*

snake/
serpiente

beans/*frijoles*

dog/*perro*

oar/*remo*

sword/*espada*

El Bumblebeeto

boat/*barco*

one/*uno*

eight/*ocho*

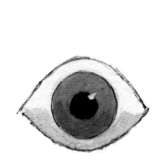

island/*isla*

river/*río*

bag/*bolso*

tree/*árbol*

Mama
Junebug
Jones

eye/*ojo*